Dear Parent:
Your child's love of reading starts here!

Every child learns to read in a different way and at his or her own speed. Some go back and forth between reading levels and read favorite books again and again. Others read through each level in order. You can help your young reader improve and become more confident by encouraging his or her own interests and abilities. From books your child reads with you to the first books he or she reads alone, there are I Can Read Books for every stage of reading:

My First

SHARED READING
Basic language, word repetition, and whimsical illustrations, ideal for sharing with your emergent reader

1

BEGINNING READING
Short sentences, familiar words, and simple concepts for children eager to read on their own

2

READING WITH HELP
Engaging stories, longer sentences, and language play for developing readers

3

READING ALONE
Complex plots, challenging vocabulary, and high-interest topics for the independent reader

4

ADVANCED READING
Short paragraphs, chapters, and exciting themes for the perfect bridge to chapter books

I Can Read Books have introduced children to the joy of reading since 1957. Featuring award-winning authors and illustrators and a fabulous cast of beloved characters, I Can Read Books set the standard for beginning readers.

A lifetime of discovery begins with the magical words **"I Can Read!"**

Visit www.icanread.com for information on enriching your child's reading experience.

Beat Bugs: In My Life

 For information address HarperCollins Children's Books, a division of HarperCollins Publishers, 195 Broadway, New York, NY 10007.
www.icanread.com

Library of Congress Control Number: 2016942116
ISBN 978-0-06-264067-3

Typography by Brenda E. Angelilli

17 18 19 20 21 SCP 10 9 8 7 6 5 4 3 2 1 ❖ First Edition

I Can Read!™ BEGINNING 1 READING

Beat Bugs™
In My Life

adapted by
Cari Meister
based on a story
written by
Josh Wakely
Beat Bugs
created by
Josh Wakely

HARPER
An Imprint of HarperCollins*Publishers*

It is Katter’s birthday.

So the Beat Bugs are having a party.

Kumi has made leaf cakes for Katter.
Katter and the Beat Bugs
are best friends!

Katter takes a bite of a cake.

"It is very good," she says.

"But I cannot eat any more.

I do not feel well."

Walter wonders
if it is because she is growing.

“Am I getting bigger?” asks Katter.

Crick pulls out his tape measure.

“Yes,” he says. “You are!”

Gurgle-glug.

"What is that?" asks Buzz.

Katter grabs her tummy.

"I am sorry.

I have to go."

“Go?” asks Kumi.

“From your own party?” asks Buzz.

Katter nods.

She needs to lie down.

Katter finds a quiet spot.

Soon she is sound asleep.

Katter is missing
her birthday party!

The Beat Bugs are sad.

They want to celebrate

Katter's birthday with her.

"Let's bring the party to her!"

says Kumi.

But where is Katter?

The Beat Bugs split up
to search for her.
They do not want Katter
to be alone on her birthday.

"Look," says Buzz.

"Katter is sleeping."

"Wake up," says Jay.

But Katter does not wake up

She sleeps for two days straight.
"This is the longest
and sleepiest
birthday party ever," says Buzz.

Finally, Katter wakes up.

“Oh my,” says Walter.

“Look. You have wings!”

“They look very pretty,” says Buzz.

Katter flaps her wings.

"I can fly," she says.

Katter is no longer a caterpillar.

She is a butterfly now.

Katter flies over the garden.

She can't believe how much

she has changed.

Nothing will ever be the same.

Except for her friends.

“You are back,” says Kumi.

“I changed,” says Katter.

“But you are still my
best-est friends.”

"And you are still
our best-est friend,"
say the Beat Bugs.

They learn it is okay to grow up,
and it is okay to change.

But they will always be
the best-est of friends.
Happy birthday, Katter!

Sing along with Katter!

"In My Life" lyrics

Written by John Lennon/Paul McCartney

There are places I remember
All my life, though some have changed,
Some forever, not for better.
Some have gone, and some remain.

All these places had their moments,
In my life I've loved them all.

But of all these friends, la la la,
There is no-one compares with you,
And these memories lose their meaning
When I think of love as something new.

Though I know I'll never lose affection
For people and things that went before,
I know I'll often stop and think about them,
In my life I love you more.

Though I know I'll never lose affection
For people and things that went before,
I know I'll often stop and think about them,
In my life I love you more.

In my life I love you more.